THE GLOOMY GHOST

THE ACCIDENTAL MONSTERS

MONSTERS

THE GLOOMY GHOST

David Lubar

AN
APPLE
PAPERBACK

SCHOLASTIC INC.
New York Toronto London Auckland Sydney

For Jon, my big brother.
Thanks for teaching me what I needed to know,
and taking me where I wanted to go.

ISBN 0-590-90721-2

12 11 10 9 8 7 6 5 4 3 2 1   8 9/9 0 1 2/0

Printed in the U.S.A.
First Scholastic printing, February 1998

CONTENTS

GETTING SPOOKED

Being little stinks. Adults act like I don't exist. Even when I'm in the room they act like I'm not there. They talk about me right in front of me. Maybe they think their words just shoot across the room and don't reach down to me. It's amazing. I can be sitting right there — right under their noses — and they'll start talking about me. Rory this and Rory that. Rory had a bad day today or Rory shouldn't be playing with that boy down the street. Sometimes I want to shout at them, "Hey, I'm right here!"

They all do it. Mom and Dad, Mr. Nordy next door, Dr. Bugwitz, my teacher Mrs. Rubric, everyone.

Being little stinks. But it's better than being dead. Being dead can *really* stink. No joke. I don't mean you start to stink. Well, I guess you do if you're really dead. But I'm just sort of dead, so I don't stink.

Maybe I'm just almost dead. But I know I'm dead enough to be a ghost.

I'm skipping over a bunch of stuff. I've got to go back, so it makes sense. It's like Mom says when I get excited. "Slow down. Just tell one thing at a time." Okay, I'm going to slow down and tell one thing at a time.

First, who am I? I'm Rory. But that doesn't tell you a lot. I'm in kindergarten. I've got a brother, Sebastian, who is really great. He's my big buddy. He lets me look at his monster books. I've got a sister, Angelina. She's the oldest. She's getting close to being a big person, so sometimes she treats me like I'm not there. But she also makes me cookies sometimes. And she was a witch for a while. Not a nasty witch, but a fun one. Angelina and Sebastian fight all the time. Not hit and punch fight, but words. Sebastian usually wins. He's cool. His friends call him Splat. That's a funny story. I'll tell it later if I remember.

I like soldiers and monsters and trucks — especially monster trucks. I like guns, but Mom doesn't. I don't have a lot of guns. I used to not have any, but I made guns out of sticks, so Mom gave up and let me have some toy guns. Dad doesn't mind if I have toy guns. I don't point them at any real people or animals — just at enemy soldiers and monsters.

Wow, I'm really chattering. If I keep talking about me, this story won't go anywhere. I'd better hurry through the rest. So, there's Sebastian and Angelina. I told you about them. I have a friend, Becky, who lives down the street. She's great. She can bend her thumb back so it touches her wrist. And she can do that trick with her eyes where she makes them go all white. Her mom hates that. I think Sebastian has a crush on Becky's big sister, Dawn. He acts real goofy when she's around.

I have another friend, Tony, who lives down the street, but the other way. Becky and Tony hate each other right now. Oh, and I've got parents. Mom and Dad. That's what I call them.

Before I got dead, I guess I was just a normal kid. I'm still a normal kid, except I'm a ghost kid. That would be cool, if I was alive. But I guess you can't be alive *and* be a ghost. It's like when Dad says *you can't have it both ways*. My parents are always saying things. Most of the time, I'm not really sure what they mean. Like, what does "some day you'll thank me for this" mean? It's more like, "Someday I'll spank you for this." That, I understand.

So anyhow, now you know enough about me. And, oh, yeah, I live in Lewington and I go to morning kindergarten at Washington Irving Elementary School. I don't know if I'll be going there anymore, since I'm dead.

Now you know everything about me except how I got into this mess. Well, I guess it really started when I broke the television.

CHAPTER 2

TOTALLY BUSHED

I figured it would be great to have the sound from the television come out of the big speakers on the stereo. My friend Tony's dad had their set hooked up that way. It didn't look hard, and the television sounded real good. I was up early in the morning and everyone else was asleep. I was bored. So I got some wire from Dad's tool bench in the garage and started trying to connect things. Really, how hard could it be?

Harder than I thought, I guess. As soon as I hooked up the first wire, there was this *ZZZZZ-AAAAP* sound and a burning smell. I jumped halfway across the room when that happened. Then a bunch of white smoke came from inside the television. It smelled awful.

"I'm dead," I said.

Dad would kill me when he found out. I didn't have to think twice about what to do. I rushed straight out of the house. There was no way I could hide what I'd done. If I'd broken something small, like a radio, I could hide it. But even if I had a place to hide the television, I couldn't move it by myself. Our television weighs a ton. There was no way I could blame someone else, either. I'd broken enough things before so they always knew, whenever anything broke, Rory did it.

The alarm clock was my fault. I'll admit that. I wanted to see how it worked. How could it always ring at the right time? But I didn't mean to break the vacuum cleaner. And I sure didn't mean to wreck both garage door openers on the same day. But all those things just sort of happened to me.

I went out the back door. There were some bushes at the corner of the yard next to the swings. They were real thick and the branches drooped to the ground. Dad kept asking Sebastian to trim them. And Sebastian kept saying he would. I crawled through the branches and hid. It was almost like being under my blankets, but there was fresh air.

I could see it now. It's always the same. First, they'd get angry. Then they'd try to figure out a reason — like if there was a reason I did it, then it wouldn't be so bad. So I'd tell them I was just trying to make it better.

"Didn't you think?" Mom would say. "Didn't you stop to think?"

"We are *very, very* disappointed with you," Dad would say.

Then they'd start in on the safety stuff.

"You could have gotten hurt." That was the one I heard the most. That's what they said when I tried to drive the car. That's what they said when I tried to cut down the old dead apple tree with Dad's hand-saw. That's what they said when I tried to teach my-self to swim in Mr. Nordy's pool. I guess I could have gotten hurt, but nothing ever seems dangerous when I start out.

Then they'd figure out my punishment. That would be bad. I mean, I'd destroyed the television. We practically lived around it. Every night, we watched TV. It was the center of our lives. And I had broken it. No doubt about it — I was dead.

Sitting under some bushes can get pretty boring. I dug around, looking for bugs to play with. I didn't find any. There's never a good bug around when you need one. I had my watch with me. Mom and Dad gave it to me for my last birthday. There aren't any hands like on the clocks at school. Those are hard to read. On my watch, the minutes are numbers. Sebas-tian taught me how to read it. He's always teaching me important stuff. I thought I'd been under the bushes for at least an hour, but it had only been two or three minutes.

Then I started getting hungry. I thought about sneaking into the kitchen for a box of cereal. But I wasn't going to leave my hiding place for a long time. I was just going to stay until they forgot about the TV. Then I'd come back. It might take a day or two, but it was my only hope.

While I was looking around for something to do, I noticed there were red berries on the bushes. Tony said that all red berries are poison. But Tony lies all the time.

Last week, Tony said, "My dad used to tame lions in the circus."

I'm pretty sure that isn't true. His dad doesn't have any scars. And he wears a suit when he goes to work. Lion tamers don't wear suits.

"I have a spaceship in my closet," Tony told me last month.

I looked. He didn't. I wish he did.

Tony also told me he was starring in a new television show. He isn't. They wouldn't let him have a show. He talks too fast and I'm just about the only one who can understand him.

He even told me he was going to have a rock group at his birthday party, but all he had was Chuckle-Buckle, the Happy Clown. I can't think of anything he ever told me that was actually true. So there was no reason to believe him about the berries. I pulled one from the bush and looked at it. Strawberries are red, and they aren't poison.

I rolled it around in my fingers. It was so small. There was no way one little berry could do anything bad to me.

I put it in my mouth.

CHAPTER
3

BERRIED ALIVE

*T*he outside of the berry didn't have any taste. I figured if it was poison it would be bitter.

I bit it.

The inside didn't have much taste, either. It was a little sour, but not too bad. I tried a couple more. By then I realized that there weren't enough to fill me up, anyhow. I'd just have to put up with being hungry. That shouldn't be a problem. A real soldier can stand anything. We can walk for days through the mud and the rain, carrying a ton of stuff. We can go forever without any water except a little sip every eight hours.

My stomach had stopped rumbling.

I wondered whether they had tried to turn on the TV yet. I could see it. Dad would switch it on and there'd be nothing. He'd thump it on top a couple of times, or maybe shake the remote. It still wouldn't turn on. So he'd call Mom. And they'd both try it. Then they'd check the plug to make sure it was in. Then they'd call Sebastian, since he's the only one in the house who knows how to use the VCR.

My stomach didn't hurt anymore. It didn't feel like anything. It was more than not feeling. It was like it never had any feeling at all.

Maybe they'd smell it first. They'd walk into the living room and smell the burnt TV smell. There'd been a pretty big puff of smoke. It probably still smelled in there. Big people can sniff stuff like that and know exactly what happened. It's amazing. The time I melted one of my tub toys with the magnifying glass, Mom knew right away what was going on. And when I'd tried to paint Dad's tires to surprise him for his birthday, he came running out to the garage before I'd even gotten the first one finished.

My legs felt funny, too. They felt like they had no feeling. I wondered if I'd been sitting one way for too long. I stretched them out. They still felt strange.

I hoped Sebastian wasn't planning to watch anything special tonight. I wouldn't want to get him mad at me, too.

"Rory?"

Someone was calling for me. It sounded like Dad. I pulled myself deeper into the bushes. I had to use my arms. My legs weren't working.

This was bad. I wondered if they'd found out about the TV already, or were just looking for me. Luckily,

I could be anywhere. There were a bunch of places for them to look. I could be at Tony's, or at Becky's, or at the playground down the street. I could be just about anywhere on the block.

My fingers started to tingle.

It won't be easy for them to find me. I'll be safe for a while. This was a real good hiding place. I only used it for big emergencies. They didn't know about it — not even Sebastian. They've never found me here. Maybe they won't turn on the television. Maybe if I got some books or magazines for everyone, they'd read instead. That might work.

My arms felt funny. I couldn't sit up anymore.

Something's wrong. I didn't feel anything anywhere. Just my face. I couldn't move.

"Mom?"

I called Mom. She could fix anything. Sometimes Sebastian calls her Doctor Mom. I tried to shout but it wasn't even a whisper. I think my lips moved. I'm not sure. They tingled for a while. But now I couldn't feel them, either. I couldn't hear anything. I couldn't see anything.

I couldn't feel myself thinking anymore. I couldn't . . .

CHAPTER 4

JUST PASSING THROUGH

Gee, I felt a lot better when I woke up. I must have fallen asleep. That was really weird. I sat up. It was brighter outside. I checked my watch. It was almost twelve o'clock. I stretched, but I didn't feel stiff. That's funny. I usually have to stretch when I wake up. Then I saw him. I don't know how he got in here with me. He was sleeping.

"Hey, wake up," I said to the other kid. What was he doing in my secret place? He looked familiar. Wow. He looked just like me. That made me feel really creepy. It was like looking in a mirror, but without the mirror. "Wake up!" I shouted at him. I decided to shake his shoulder. I tried to do it. But I couldn't touch him. My hand just couldn't get close.

Maybe it was time to find another place to hide. I started to push my way through the bushes.

But the bushes went through me.

They just went right through my arm.

"Mom!"

I shouted without thinking. I didn't care about the television anymore. I just wanted my mom. I ran toward the house.

Sebastian stepped out the back door. "Rory," he called.

"Here," I waved my arms and shouted. I ran toward him. But he just looked around, like I wasn't even there. Maybe he was so mad he was going to ignore me. But that didn't make any sense. Why was he calling me if he was going to ignore me?

I ran to the steps. I tried to run up them, but I went through them. I was in the steps, up to my chest. It was like I'd been cut in half. Sebastian was right in front of me. His shoes were right in front of my eyes.

"SEBASTIAN!" I shouted as hard and as loud as I could. He tilted his head for a second. I think he almost heard me. I shouted again. And again. He stood for a moment. I kept shouting. I shouted so hard I knew my face was red. My brother turned around and went inside.

I looked down. I was half in the porch. I didn't like that. Seeing my body cut off that way made me shiver. I lifted my hand. It came right up through the old boards with the chipped gray paint. No, I didn't like being inside something. I stepped back. I got out of the porch.

I looked behind me, at the bushes. The kid in there . . . No, it couldn't be.

I knew the answer. "I'm dreaming," I said. It was that simple. I'd fallen asleep, and this was a bad dream. It had to be. I couldn't really walk through the porch. I laughed at myself for being fooled by a dream.

All I had to do was wake myself up. That was easy. "Hey, wake up!" I shouted.

It didn't work. I tried again. It still didn't work. No matter how loud I got, I didn't wake up.

Maybe I could wake the kid in the bushes. But something about him scared me a little. I sort of had an idea who he was, but I didn't want to think about it. Sooner or later, I knew someone would come along and tell me what to do. Adults ignore kids a lot of the time, but they never let them alone for too long. I decided to walk around to the front of the house. Maybe I could get inside from there since the porch didn't have a lot of steps.

That's when I saw the puppy. He was in the yard by the side of the house, wandering around like he was lost. "Puppy," I called to him. "Here, boy." I was afraid he'd act like Sebastian and ignore me. But he turned and looked. Then he ran toward me. As he ran through the grass, I noticed he wasn't running over the grass. He was really running through it, just like the way I went through the bushes.

"Hi," I said when he reached me. I bent down to

pet him. I was scared my hand would go right through him, but it didn't. It was like sticking my hand out the car window when the car is going fast. Something pushed against my hand, but it was almost like air. But the puppy loved it. He wagged his tail and begged for more when I stopped.

He looked like Browser, Mr. Nordy's dog, only a lot smaller. I remembered that Mr. Nordy had another dog staying with him for a while. Her name was Sheila. The puppy looked like her, too.

"What's going on, puppy?" I asked. I didn't really expect an answer, and I didn't get one. But at least I wasn't alone now. I bent down and picked up the puppy. Then I went toward the front of the house.

I ran into trouble before I got there.

CHAPTER
5

THAT SINKING SENSATION

As I walked toward the front of the house, I started thinking about the television again. Even though I had bigger problems, I couldn't help myself. I could just see Mom and Dad shouting and shaking their heads.

I didn't notice anything for the first couple of steps. But then I realized I was getting shorter. I'm not that tall to start with, so it made a big difference. And it was worse than that. I only thought I was getting shorter.

Instead, I was sinking into the ground.

This was as bad as walking through the porch. I took another step forward, and sank deeper. I tried stepping backward. It didn't matter. I still sank. My legs were deep enough that I couldn't even see my foot when I took a step.

The ground came up to my chest. I didn't want to

let go of the puppy, but I was afraid I'd drag him under the ground, so I put him down. He ran in a circle around me, barking and leaping all over the place.

"How come you aren't sinking?" I asked him.

He ran over and licked my face.

"If you can walk on the ground, so can I." I took a step. I rose a bit higher. I took another step. It seemed to be okay. I was coming back out of the ground. I was halfway around the side of the house now.

Oh, no! I just remembered that it was Saturday. Sebastian's favorite show — *Monster Mayhem* — was on tonight. And the TV was broken. I'd really messed things up.

And I was sinking again.

I was back up to my chest.

The puppy thought this was great. I didn't. There had to be a reason. And I had to find it fast. Even though I wasn't walking, I was still sinking.

I was up to my chin.

Think, I told myself.

I lifted my hands over my head and tried to stand on my tiptoes, but it didn't make a difference. My mouth sank under and then my nose. That's when I realized I wasn't breathing. My eyes would be next, and I really really didn't want them under the ground.

Think harder!

I figured it out just as the ground reached the top

of my cheeks. Every time I thought about what I'd done wrong — breaking the you-know-what — I sank down. I needed to think about something else. It wasn't easy.

Dad has a joke where he says, "Quick, don't think about purple alligators." Of course, as soon as he says it, I can't help thinking about purple alligators.

But Mrs. Rubric is always saying, "Rory, try to think before you speak."

And it's easy to talk without thinking. I'm *really* good at that. So I started talking to the puppy, telling him all about myself, as we walked to the front of the house.

"I like monsters," I told him. "My favorite is Frankenstein's monster. Most kids just call him Frankenstein. That's wrong. Frankenstein is the doctor who made the monster. Sebastian taught me that. He's my big brother. You'd like him. He has a poster of Frankenstein's monster in his room. I want one, too, but Mom says *no* because it would give me nightmares. So I go look at his." I really liked that poster. It was big and scary and great. I didn't like to look at it if I was alone, but I loved to look at it with Sebastian.

It worked. With each step, I went up a little. By the time we got to the front door, I was walking on the ground again.

The porch only came up to my knees when I

walked across it, so that wasn't a big problem. I reached for the knob and my hand went right through it. I realized I could probably just walk in. As I got ready to try, I heard my parents talking inside.

"Where could he be?" Mom asked.

"Calm down," Dad said. "I'm sure he's hiding because of the television. What did you expect him to do?"

Oh, boy. They'd found it. When I heard that, I started to sink again. I had to get that thought out of my mind right away. I started to sing a song. "Twinkle, twinkle, little star."

That did the trick. I took a step back from the house. I wanted to go inside, because Mom and Dad were there and they could fix anything that I'd done to myself. But I knew that if I went in now, I wouldn't hear about anything except *that broken thing*, and I'd be in big trouble if I kept thinking about it.

I had to go somewhere else for help.

"YIP!" The puppy barked at me. I guess he was annoyed that I wasn't paying attention to him. I looked down at him and had an idea. I knew where I could go for help.

It wasn't cold outside. I couldn't feel the temperature, but I could see from the sunshine that it was warm. Even so, the idea I had made me shiver. I felt like my whole body had just been dipped in ice water. Worse, after being dipped, I'd been lifted out into a cold wind. And had a bunch of snowballs thrown at me, while I ate a Popsicle.

Shivering or not, I knew where I had to go.

CHAPTER 6

HAUNT AND SEEK

People are always trying to hide things from kids. They seem to think we can't stand bad news. But that's not true. I realized what my bad news was. I'd become a ghost.

"I'm a ghost," I said out loud, just to make sure that I knew. If my parents were breaking the news to me, they would have dragged it out for hours.

"Rory," Mom would have said, "did you ever think how special it would be if you could walk through walls?"

Then Dad would add, "Don't you just love that Christmas story with all the ghosts? You know, the one with Scrooge and Tiny Tim. Isn't that a great story?"

I didn't hide the news. There wasn't any reason to. "I'm a ghost," I said again, just to make sure I believed myself.

So that was the bad news. But I wasn't the only ghost. The puppy was also a ghost. If I was a ghost and he was a ghost, that meant there had to be other ghosts. All I had to do was find them. They'd help me. Then I could get back into my body and be a kid again.

I just needed to go to the best place for ghosts. That was easy. Everybody in town knew where that was. We called it the Winston House. I guess the guy who used to own it was named Winston. I really don't know much about that, but I do know that it's haunted. Everybody says so. Tony said he'd seen ghosts there, but that doesn't count. Even so, lots of other kids say it's haunted, so it has to be.

You could see the top half of the Winston House from here. It's over on the hill behind the main part of town. It's real creepy to look at. But that's not surprising, since it's haunted.

"Come on, puppy," I said, "let's go for a walk."

At the word *walk*, he started jumping and yipping. "I have to stop calling you puppy," I said. "How about a name?"

He wagged his tail, so I guess he liked the idea. Sebastian had read me these fun books about two ghost kids who were twins and had a ghost dog. That dog had a great name, but I didn't want to steal it. I wanted to come up with my own name.

The puppy yipped again. That seemed like a good name. "How about Yip?" I asked him.

He agreed.

I guess it seemed silly for me to talk with the puppy like that, but it kept my mind off other things. I might look brave marching right over to the haunted house, but I didn't feel brave. I felt scared and alone. But I knew I had to do something. I was in all kinds of trouble, and nobody was going to come along and help me.

I'd walked about five blocks when I saw Norman in front of his house. He was standing there looking down the street like he was waiting for something. He's Sebastian's friend. But he's my friend, too. He doesn't treat me like a kid. Norman is really smart. He knows everything. Maybe he could help me.

"Norman," I called, running up to him. "Hey, Norman. I'm a ghost."

Norman took a step and walked right through me.

It was weird, because it didn't feel like anything. For a second, when his body passed through my head, I saw inside him. But it was real dark, and I think I closed my eyes. I wish I'd closed my ears. I *heard* his heart. It sounded all squishy and wet.

"Norman," I called as he walked away.

He didn't stop. It was hard to remember that people couldn't hear me. I was used to being seen. I'd been visible all my life. Well, I was invisible to adults sometimes, but they could still see me if they had to. I tried again.

"NORMAN!" I shouted.

He paused and looked around, then said, "How peculiar. I appear to be having an auditory hallucination. Not unusual, considering the number of synapses in the cerebral cortex. I'm sure it's nothing to worry about."

I had no idea what that meant. "NORMAN!" I shouted again. This time, he didn't even stop or look around. He ran down the street toward the mailman who was coming this way. I guess he was waiting for a package or something.

I turned back toward the Winston House. I'm not supposed to cross the street by myself. That's one of the big rules. There are lots of rules, but only a couple of big ones. Those are the ones that, if you don't listen, you could get hurt. Don't play with matches. Don't talk to strangers. Don't get anyone in the Mellon family angry with you.

I guess the big rules didn't count right now. Even so, it felt funny walking across a street without holding anybody's hand. Then Yip ran ahead and a car came at him. I screamed. The car went right through Yip without hitting him. He wasn't hurt at all.

Even though I knew I couldn't be hurt, either, I didn't want to get hit. So I raced over and grabbed Yip and hurried to the other side of the street. I guess I was really a chicken crossing the road. That made me laugh.

I kept feeling happy all the way across town, until

I got close to the hill. Then I walked up the hill, watching the Winston House growing bigger and bigger. It almost looked like a little castle. There were three floors. I could tell that from the windows. One corner had a round part — I don't know what they call it. That's what made me think of a castle. The old brown paint was pretty faded, and a lot of it had fallen off. By now, I was so close I had to bend my head back to see the top of the house.

"It's daytime," I said. "Nothing scary happens in the daytime."

Boy, was that a lie. Look how much had happened to me already since I got up this morning.

But I had another idea. "I'm a ghost," I said. "Nothing can hurt me."

Boy, was that a lie, too. I thought about sinking into the ground, and just knew that even when you're a ghost, bad things can happen.

"It's just other ghosts in there," I said, looking ahead at the Winston House. "A ghost would never hurt another ghost."

I wondered whether that was the biggest lie of all. It was like saying a kid would never hurt another kid, or an adult would never hurt another adult. Kids hurt kids all the time. There was a bully in my class, so I knew about getting hurt. And if adults didn't hurt other adults, we wouldn't need police officers and soldiers. But we have lots of them.

Stop talking, I said to myself, *and get going.*

I walked up to the Winston House. For as long as I could remember, it had been empty. Nobody lived there. Nobody who was alive, at least. Right now, as I stood in the front yard, I could hear voices inside — a whole bunch of voices.

I walked up the steps. When I realized what I was doing, I was so surprised I stopped and looked down. Back home, I'd gone right through the porch. Maybe the Winston House was so haunted it was like a ghost itself. I bent and touched the porch. I couldn't push my hand through it, but I didn't really feel anything.

I went up the rest of the steps and knocked on the door. Nobody came, but the door swung open. It made a spooky creaking sound, and I almost turned and ran. Even with the sun shining, the sound scared me. Yip trotted ahead. I guess he didn't know that this was a scary place. I followed him.

There were people inside. I saw four people in a living room. Two men were sitting, reading books, and a man and a woman were talking. They were dressed differently. One of the men who was reading had ancient clothes, like someone from Pilgrim times. He was sitting in a plain, old wood rocking chair. The woman and the other man with a book had old clothes, but not as old as the Pilgrim. The man who was talking to the woman had normal stuff. The two of them were next to each other on a couch.

"Hi," I called.

Nobody looked up.

"Hey. Can you hear me?" I shouted.

They didn't pay any attention to me. I walked into the middle of the room. They had to be ghosts. This was a haunted house, and I was sure that nobody could see them. Nobody who was alive, that is. I went up to the woman.

"Excuse me," I said. I tapped her on the shoulder. She felt like Yip — that same feeling of being there, but being made of nothing. I was sure she was a ghost.

Even so, she paid no attention to me.

"Excuse me," I said again. "Can you help me?" I felt another shiver run through me. I wasn't afraid of her — I was afraid she couldn't hear me. What if nobody — not even other ghosts — could hear me? I couldn't imagine ever being that alone.

Finally, she looked over. "Just a minute. I'm busy right now. Can't you see we're talking?"

"Sorry." I backed up and waited, but I could tell right away that she'd forgotten all about me. I looked at the man she was talking to. He didn't notice me, either.

I walked over to the Pilgrim guy, but I realized he'd never help me. I'd learned that in school. The Pilgrims were always saying, "Children should be seen and not heard."

Mrs. Rubric told us about that on the first day of school. Then, whenever we were talking, she'd say, "Now, class, let's all be good little Pilgrims."

Yip was running around, sniffing at everything, but they didn't pay any attention to him, either. I went over to the last guy in the room. "Mister?" I said.

He held a finger to his lips and said, "Shush. Can't you see I'm reading. Whatever your question is, I'm sure it can wait."

"But — " I was getting tired of this.

"Shush! Now be a good boy and run along and play."

I walked into the hallway. There was someone in the next room. It was a woman. Maybe she'd help me. As I walked in, she screamed.

I jumped back. I expected to feel my heart pounding, but there was nothing like that inside me. My body was quiet.

The woman clenched her fists and screamed again. Then she fell to the ground.

I didn't know what to do. I wanted to run. But I also wanted to help her. Before I could do anything, she got up. She screamed again. And she fell again.

And again.

I turned and ran down the hall, heading toward the door. I didn't care if there were answers here. The place was too creepy.

"You're new."

I stopped and looked up toward the voice. There was a girl standing on the stairs. She was about Angelina's age, but dressed like someone in those pictures from before there were cars and everyone rode around the cities in wagons.

She came down a step. "Yes, you're new. But you aren't dead yet."

"What?" I stared up at her as she came down the rest of the steps.

She reached out and put a hand on my forehead, almost like Mom does when I have a fever. Except Mom's hand feels cool when I have a temperature. This hand didn't feel cold or hot.

"An hour," she said. Then she frowned and moved her hand a little like she was searching for something. "No, two hours. Yes, you have two hours. I'm sure of it." She sighed and added, "I do so wish we had flowers here. I haven't seen flowers in ages."

"What do you mean?" I didn't understand what she was talking about. "Two hours for what?"

"That's how much life your body has left," she said. She smiled and closed her eyes. "You look very peaceful, lying there. Yes, two hours. If nobody finds you . . ."

"After that?" I asked.

"Then you'll be dead for good, and you'll never be able to go back. But you can come here." She let her hand drop from my forehead. "Could you bring me flowers?" she asked.

I turned and ran from the house. As I rushed down the steps, I looked at my watch. It was four-thirteen. If I didn't get someone to find my body, I'd be dead by six-thirteen — dead forever.

8

THE SPIRITS ARE ABOUT TO SPEAK

I ran down the street. Yip ran with me. He was having a lot of fun. I wasn't. When I got to the bottom of the hill, I saw something that made me stop.

"That's it," I said. There was a house with a sign in the window. I couldn't read all of the words — I'm just learning a little bit of that right now. They aren't teaching it in school yet, but Sebastian's been showing me some words. I know how to read *house* and *car* and *vampire*. And I know *Frankenstein* from Sebastian's poster. That didn't help. Those words weren't on the sign in the window. But there was a picture of a hand and a crystal ball. I knew what that meant — there was a fortune-teller here. Maybe she'd be able to see me.

I was so excited, I ran right through the door. Inside, there was a woman sitting at a table. She had a scarf on her head and big earrings. She was staring into a crystal ball. Another woman, who looked like a grandmother, sat on the other side of the table. This was great. I knew I'd come to the right place.

The woman with the earrings waved her hand over the crystal ball, then looked up at the other woman and said, "You were wise to come to Madam Zonga. I know all. I see all. I can speak with the spirits."

Boy, was this a relief. I ran up to her and said, "Hi!"

"I hear the spirits speaking," Madam Zonga said.

"Yeah. That's me. Rory. I need help." It felt so good to be able to talk to someone, I jumped up and down and clapped my hands together. This was super lucky. I could tell her about my body under the bushes, and then she could call Mom and Dad. I wouldn't have to stay dead.

"What do the spirits say?" the other woman asked.

"Oh, this is terrible." Madam Zonga gasped and clenched her fists. "They tell me you have a curse on your money."

"What?" I didn't know what she was talking about. "That's not what I said." Maybe she was talking to other spirits. I looked around the room, but there was nobody else there.

"Yes," Madam Zonga said, "they are very clear about this. And they are worried about you. There is a terrible curse." She closed her eyes for a moment and shuddered.

I turned away from her and ran over to the woman. "I didn't say anything about money. I ate some berries and I'm gonna die. Help me."

She didn't hear me, either. "A curse?" she said. She hunched up in her chair like she was trying to hide. "Can you help me?"

"Of course," Madam Zonga said. She raised a finger to her lips to make the other woman be quiet. Then she stared into the crystal ball again for a minute. "The spirits are guiding me. They have told me what to do. You must take all of your money from the bank and bring it to me this evening. Wrap it in a handkerchief — a plain white handkerchief. With the help of the spirits, I will remove the curse."

"You can do that?" the lady asked.

"I will try my best," Madam Zonga said. She reached out and held the other woman's arm. "It is very dangerous for me to try, but I must help you."

"Thank you. Thank you very much." The woman stood up and hurried out the door.

"What spirits?" I said to Madam Zonga.

She got out of her chair as soon as the lady left. Then she went through a curtain to another room and picked up the phone. "Hi," she said to the person on the other end. "It's me. I got a good one. We'll make enough to get out of town. Get packed up. I want to be out of here tonight, before she realizes we have her money."

She hung up. Then she laughed.

When I saw Madam Zonga laughing I got so angry, I tried to hit the table, but my fist went right through it. "You liar! You cheater!" I screamed. She didn't hear anything. "You're just a big fat fake!"

Yip growled at her. She didn't notice.

It was no use. She couldn't hear either of us. I raced out of there. I had to get home. But I was so angry, I could hardly think. Calm down, I told myself. I took a deep breath, even though I didn't need to breathe, then I took a couple of steps. As I walked toward the curb, a van came by. It slowed down. There was something turning around and around on the top of the van. It looked like some kind of antenna. The van stopped.

I took another really deep breath. That was better. I was hardly angry at all. The van drove past me and went down the road.

I realized I could get home quicker if I took a shortcut. I didn't have to go along the streets. I could just go straight toward my house. Instead of walking around Hutchin's Department Store on the corner, I went through it.

Yip followed right along. I didn't worry about anything in front of me. I just walked. When I came out of the other side of the store, I kept going straight toward my house. I went through parked cars and trees and the bookstore and the shoe store.

Then I walked right through a house. At first, I started to go through the porch, but then I learned something. If I really looked where I was walking, I could go up steps. But I had to pay attention and remind myself that they were there. If I walked without looking, I went through the steps. After I came out of that house, I went through another. I was walking through the next house after that when I heard something that made me stop.

"All aboard!" a voice shouted.

I knew that voice. It was Becky. I looked around and I realized where I was right away. I was in the middle of her house, in the living room. I followed the voice to the playroom. Becky was there with a train set. That's right — I remembered something. Today was her birthday.

"Great trains," I said.

She didn't hear me. That's okay. But they really were great trains. I wish I had a set like that. Becky was running them around in a big loop. Besides the train and the track, she had some tiny houses and trees and a couple of cows.

She had lots of extra train cars, too. I watched while she added cars, making the train longer and longer. It was really great. She didn't just hook up the cars. She made the train do it. She'd put a new car behind the train, then have the train go backward. When it bumped into the next car, everything got hooked together. Then she'd make it go forward around the track.

Yip barked and chased after the trains. He kept

trying to pick them up in his mouth. It was funny. I wanted to play with them, too, but seeing Becky play with them was almost as good. Maybe I could ask for a train set for Christmas. Of course, I'd have to be alive to ask for it.

Alive!

I looked at my watch. It was five-twenty-seven. I'd been watching the trains and I'd forgotten all about getting home. Now, I only had — I tried to figure it out, but I couldn't. I just knew it wasn't a lot of minutes.

"I gotta go," I said to Becky as I rushed out of her house.

HAS ANYBODY FOUND
MY BODY?

When I got home, I ran around to the backyard to see if my body was still there. It was. I tried to grab my legs so I could drag myself out from under the bushes, but I couldn't put my hands on me.

Maybe I could get someone inside to find me. I think Sebastian had almost heard me before when I'd shouted. Maybe people in a family can sort of hear ghosts. I went to the porch and walked carefully up the steps. The back door goes right into the kitchen. That's good, because I didn't want to go anywhere near the living room. Even thinking about the living room, where the you-know-what was, made me start to sink into the floor a little.

Mom was in the kitchen, walking back and forth, saying, "Where could he be? This isn't like him to run off."

Dad was sitting at the table. "Rory's fine," he said.

"I'm sure he's just afraid to come home. But it'll start to get dark soon and he'll come back."

I tried to make them hear me. "LOOK UNDER THE BUSHES!" I shouted. But they didn't hear anything at all.

Maybe Angelina or Sebastian would hear me. I went up the stairs. At first, I couldn't find them. I thought they'd be in their own rooms. But they were both sitting in my room, looking real sad. "Hey, I'm okay," I said. "You just have to find me."

Sebastian sort of frowned, then said, "I know he's okay. I just know it."

Angelina nodded. "Yeah. I sort of feel that, too. But I wish he'd come back. I'm worried."

I heard a doorbell, then footsteps. Norman came up the hall and into my room. "Look, I got a new set of magnets," he said, holding up a box. He reached in and held up two big bars of metal. "Check this out." He put one magnet on the rug, then he moved the other near it. The first one slid away. I'd seen that before. I have some tiny plastic dogs that do the same thing. The heads push each other away, but the head sticks to the tail.

"Not now," Sebastian told him. "We've got problems."

"What's wrong?" Norman asked.

Sebastian looked down at the floor for a moment, then said, "Rory is missing."

"Oh, no." Norman picked up his magnets and

dropped them back in the box. "Have you looked for him?"

"We've been looking all day," Sebastian said. "I went everywhere — to the school and the park and the mall. And all around the neighborhood. Dad's been driving all over town. He just came back a couple of minutes ago. And he called the police, and they're looking, too."

The police? Wow. Oh, wow. I felt that big guilty feeling, when you know you've been really really really bad. The police were looking for me. As bad as that was, I realized it was also good. Maybe they'd find me. But they hadn't yet. Nobody had found me. It was those stupid bushes. If I wasn't under there, they'd see me. But my hiding place was just too good.

I looked at my watch. Oh, no. It was five-forty-nine. That's real close to being six-thirteen. I ran back down the stairs and out to the yard. I wanted to drag myself out so they'd find me and take care of me and I wouldn't have to stay dead. But that wouldn't work. I couldn't touch myself. I couldn't move myself.

No. That was wrong. I was so excited when I realized what to do, I shouted, "I GOT IT!"

With Yip chasing along behind me, I ran to the bushes. It would work. It had to.

CHAPTER 10

REPULSIVE RORY

*I*t was true — I couldn't touch myself. But that didn't mean I couldn't move myself. It meant I *could* move myself. It was just like with the magnets. At least, I hoped it was. There was some kind of force keeping me from putting my ghost hand on my real body.

If it worked like magnets, it would save me. If it didn't, I was in big trouble.

I went to the back of the bushes and tried to touch my shoulders. The closer my hands got, the more I felt something pushing me away. But I just kept pushing back harder. I got on my knees and really pushed harder than I'd ever pushed in my life. Or after my life.

"Move," I grunted as I pushed.

I moved.

What I mean is, my body moved. I slid. Just a tiny

bit at first. But I kept pushing, and my body kept sliding. I was slowly moving out from under the bushes.

It was hard at first. I really had to push. Once I got myself moving, it was a little easier. Moving my body was like sliding a heavy box across the floor. The funny thing was that I didn't feel tired. I could push forever. I sure hoped I didn't end up having to do anything forever. I could still see that woman in my mind — the one in the haunted house who was screaming and falling down over and over. ·

"I did it," I said as I realized my body was mostly out from under the bushes. But I kept pushing until I was all the way out. I didn't want to take any chance that they wouldn't find me. Then, just to be sure, I pushed myself closer to the middle of the yard, next to where I'd left my bike. It's a two-wheeler. I learned how to ride it last month.

I checked my watch. It was five-fifty-eight. I just needed to get Mom and Dad to find my body. I looked up at the house. Someone was staring down at me from Angelina's bedroom window. It was Darling. She's Angelina's cat.

I wondered if she could see me. Cats were always looking at things. They'd sit in the middle of a room and stare at something that wasn't there. Or maybe it was there, and nobody else could see it. I ran back toward the house and up the porch steps. I got so excited, I almost ran through the steps again.

Yip chased after me. "No, you'd better stay out," I said. I was afraid he'd scare Darling.

Yip ran back into the yard. I went inside the house.

"Here, kitty," I called, walking into Angelina's room.

Darling stared at me. The dark part of her eyes got bigger, like when I play with her with a string. Then she jumped down from the windowsill and walked across the carpet.

"Good girl. Come on." I hoped she'd come. Sometimes cats just do what they want. Actually, I think they do what they want all the time — and once in a while what they want is what you want, so you think they're doing it for you.

But she followed me out to the hall. I went along the hallway, leading her toward the stairs. We went past my room, where Sebastian and Angelina and Norman were sitting.

Darling looked over and went, "Mrewwww."

"Do you want to go out?" Angelina asked.

"Merrowwwll," Darling said.

"Come on," I called to her. I had to get her to the back door. It wouldn't work if Darling led Angelina to the front. I went down the stairs. Darling followed. I got her to follow me through the kitchen.

"Here you go," Angelina said. She opened the door and let Darling out.

"LOOK IN THE YARD!" I shouted.

Angelina was still looking down at Darling. She started to close the door.

"LOOK!" I shouted again.

She wasn't looking. It had all been wasted. She'd never see me out there. The door was almost closed. I checked my watch. It was six-oh-three. Even I could figure out that kind of math. I only had ten minutes left.

I could scream and shout, but it wouldn't do any good. Angelina would never hear me or see me. There was only one other thing I could try. It was a mean, rotten thing to do, but it was my only chance.

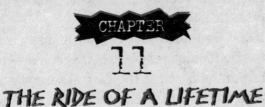

CHAPTER 11

THE RIDE OF A LIFETIME

"Yip," I called. "Get the cat, Yip."

I felt really bad. I liked Darling. But if she could see me, then she could see Yip.

And she sure could see him. He started to bark and run across the yard toward her. But he wasn't growling — he was wagging his tail. It looked like he wanted to play.

Darling sure didn't want to play. She looked back at Yip, hissed, then went dashing toward the edge of the yard by the big oak tree.

"Darling," Angelina shouted. There was no way she wouldn't hear the yowling. She opened the door again and stepped onto the porch.

She started to chase after her cat. She'd only gotten halfway down the steps when she saw me. I mean, she saw my body lying there. She froze for a second. Then she screamed, "MOM!" and went racing across the lawn.

Mom and Dad were out the door in just a couple of seconds. Dad didn't even use the steps — he just leaped from the porch to the yard. There was a lot of screaming and shouting. But then Mom ran back into the kitchen and called the emergency number.

I was so happy, I didn't notice anything wrong at first. They'd found me. I was going to be okay.

I jumped up. But I didn't come down. I was starting to float away. "Hey!" I shouted when I realized my feet weren't on the ground.

I looked at my watch. It was six-eleven. I counted out loud, "Eleven, twelve, thirteen." I had three minutes. No, it was eleven right now, so I only had two minutes. But I think I was already starting to become a real and forever ghost because the time was getting close.

I didn't want to be a ghost forever.

The ambulance came. People with white shirts and pants were running all over.

They put a mask on my face, just like on television. Then they put a needle in my arm. I really hated to watch that. But it did something good to me. I came back down. I wasn't floating anymore. I guess they were keeping me alive.

"Yip," I said, grabbing the dog and giving him a hug. "I'll be okay. They'll make me better."

They put my body on a stretcher and took me to

the ambulance. I went with them and got inside. I'd never been in an ambulance. Yip jumped out of my arms and went chasing after Darling again.

Before I could follow him, the ambulance started to drive off. I wanted to get him, but I had a funny feeling I should stay with my body. I looked back and saw everyone following in Dad's car. They raced along right behind the ambulance.

We were really racing, too, with the lights and the siren and everything. It was pretty exciting. I couldn't wait to tell Becky all about it. I wish I could take the ambulance to show-and-tell at school, but I don't think they'll let me do that.

At the hospital, more people rushed out to meet the ambulance and they got me inside really quickly. There were doctors and nurses all around me and they were doing all kinds of stuff with needles and tubes and wires. The doctors were shouting lots of things with real big words that sounded just the way Norman talks. I couldn't understand any of it.

I didn't want to watch. It felt really funny seeing them doing all that stuff to me. I figured I'd just walk around for a while. They'd make me better even if I didn't stand there and watch. I wondered what it would feel like to go back into my body. Maybe it would be like going to sleep again. Then I'd wake up and everything would be fine. I hoped that's what it would be like. I guess I'd find out soon enough.

Then I thought of something really scary. What if

they fixed me, and my body woke up and was all better, but my ghost stayed outside?

No. I didn't want to think about that. No way. That was almost as bad as thinking about breaking the you-know-what.

I walked out of the little room where they were taking care of me. I realized something else. It didn't smell like a hospital. There wasn't any smell at all. I tried to remember whether I'd smelled anything at all since I became a ghost. I didn't think so. Even when I'd hugged Yip, there hadn't been any puppy smell.

The hallway was crowded. There were a lot of people in the hospital.

Then I realized it wasn't just people. As I looked around, I saw that there weren't just doctors and nurses and patients in the hospital. There were also ghosts. Lots of ghosts.

CHAPTER 12

HOSPITAL HOSPITALITY

*T*here was a man pacing up and down the hallway. I knew he was a ghost because all the doctors and nurses walked right through him.

I ran up to him and said, "Hi. Can you hear me?" I didn't really need to talk to anyone, since I was being fixed up and wouldn't be a ghost much longer, but I guess I just wanted to talk, anyhow.

The man glanced down at me, then shook his head and looked away. "My car. My poor car," he said. "It's wrecked. They'll never be able to fix it. The whole thing is wrecked."

"It's just a car," I said. But it didn't look like he'd heard me. I walked down the hall a bit more. There were three older kids — two boys and a girl. They looked like they were in high school. Sometimes high school kids scare me, because they're so big. But I figured it was okay to talk to them here in the hospital.

"Hi," I said.

"It's your fault," the girl was shouting at one of the boys.

"I'm Rory," I told them.

"Hey," the boy shouted back at the girl, "don't blame me. I didn't drink that much."

I tried a little more to talk to them, but they were so busy shouting at each other and blaming each other, that it was no use.

There was a woman down the hall from them. She didn't want to talk to me, either. Neither did the next two men I saw. They were all busy with their own problems. And I guess they were all just used to ignoring kids. I'm not going to be like that when I grow up. When I'm an adult, I'm going to listen to every little kid who ever talks to me.

It didn't matter if they ignored me. As soon as the doctors fixed me, I'd be able to talk to Becky and Tony and all my other friends. I might even be glad to see that bully, Pit Mellon, even though he stole one of my action figures last week. He pushed everyone around because he's bigger and stronger. It wasn't fair. No, I changed my mind — I wouldn't be glad to see Pit.

I'd been wandering around for a long time. I checked my watch. It was seven-fifty-three. I decided to go back and see if the doctors were almost finished fixing me. I figured it would probably be a good idea for me to be near my body when that happened. I went back down the hall. Even though I knew it was no use, I said hi to all the other ghosts. That's just the way I am. I like saying hi to people. They didn't pay any attention to me. Boy, was I getting used to that.

When I got back to the place where I was, I wasn't there. I mean, I was gone. The room was empty. I looked around to make sure it was the right place. It was. I remembered the poster on the wall, and the big machine in the corner with all the knobs and buttons.

Don't get scared, I told myself. I had to be somewhere. I knew they must have moved me. I'd seen that on television. They bring people to the emergency room, then they move them so other people can get helped.

I ran down the hall, looking in all the rooms. I wasn't in any of them. I went up the stairs and started looking there. But the next floor was just X-ray machines and stuff like that.

So I went up another floor. Right away, I saw Sebastian and Angelina. They were sitting in this place that had a bunch of chairs. There was a table with magazines on it, too. I guess it was a waiting room. There was a big door behind them. When I walked up to the door, I could see Mom and Dad inside. I went through.

I saw myself in a bed. I looked away. There were still lots of needles and tubes in me.

A doctor was talking to Mom and Dad. "We're running tests," the doctor said.

"How is he?" Mom asked.

The doctor shook his head. "We're trying our best, but we have no idea what caused this. We're running every test we can think of. Unless we find out very soon . . ." He stopped and shook his head again.

"BERRIES!" I shouted at them. "I ate poison berries! You just have to look. They're right on the bush where you found me."

"How long?" Dad asked.

"Twelve hours," the doctor said.

"All you have to do is look," I said.

Dad shook his head. "I knew he was too young for that bike. It's all my fault. He must have hit his head when he fell. I told him to wear his helmet."

"I wasn't on my bike," I said. Then I remembered how I had pushed myself away from the bushes and out into the middle of the yard — right next to the bike.

They'd never figure out about the berries. Not unless I found some way to tell them.

13

GETTING THROUGH
IS HARD TO DO

There had to be some way to let them know about the berries. But they couldn't see me or hear me. And I couldn't touch anything. My hands went through everything. No. That wasn't true. I realized there was one thing I could touch — sort of. I could move myself. Maybe I could make my hands move. It would be like playing that game where you make people guess words just by using your hands.

I went over to my body. I really didn't like looking at me, on the hospital bed. My face was so pale, it looked like my real body was the ghost. But I had to do something. I put my hand through the bed under my body's hand. Then I started to push. It was almost like I was playing with a Rory puppet. That idea made me laugh.

Even better — it was working. My whole arm started to move up from the bed.

That's when everything went crazy all at once. BEEEEEEP! An alarm started screeching and things started ringing and flashing and the doctor bent over me and the nurses came running in and Mom and Dad started shouting questions.

I jumped away from my body.

The alarms stopped.

"Some kind of stress," the doctor said, shaking his head. "Something was putting an extra burden on his system."

"What?" Dad asked.

"I wish I knew," the doctor said. "I've seen it happen before, especially in unconscious patients, but we've never been able to explain it. Just be thankful it stopped so quickly. Sometimes, it doesn't stop at all. And then, we're in serious trouble."

I stepped back some more, just to be safe. I guess I couldn't take any chances trying to move myself again. But what else could I do? At least I had more time. Before, I just had two hours. And I'd saved myself. This time, I had twelve hours. I checked my watch. It was eight-oh-five. At night. That was easy to figure out. Twelve hours would be eight-oh-five again, but in the morning.

I jumped as I felt someone tugging on my arm.

"Hey, come on. Answer me."

I looked down. There was a little kid next to me — one of those real little ones who aren't even in kindergarten yet. I think he might have been talking for a while. I'd heard something, but I hadn't paid any attention to it. I had my own problems.

"Come on," the kid said again. "Talk to me."

I didn't have time for this. I needed to tell Mom and Dad about the berries. There had to be a way. I looked down at the kid and told him, "I can't talk to you right now. I've got problems."

"That's what everyone says. You big people are all alike," he said. Then he stomped his foot. It was kind of funny, since it didn't make any sound. I guess I laughed.

"It's not funny," he shouted. He turned and walked out.

You big people? I thought about that ghost in the hall, who just kept talking about his car. And I thought about all the other big ghosts who didn't notice me.

"Wait!" I called, running after him. "Wait up. I'm sorry. I didn't mean to laugh at you."

He stopped. I ran up to him and said, "I'm Rory. What's your name?"

"Scott," he said. "I'm real sick. Are you?"

"Yeah. I ate some red berries," I told him.

"Wow. You're kidding? Those are poison. Everybody knows that."

"I guess so. What happened to you?"

Scott shrugged. "I got some kind of disease. I don't know what it's called. My parents don't talk about it. They never tell me anything. I wish they would. But all they ever do is whisper about it."

"That's rough," I said. Except for now, I'd never been really sick. I had the chicken pox once, but that wasn't so bad. Mostly, I just had to stay in bed that time, and Mom bought me a bunch of coloring books and a new box of crayons. "I hope you get better."

He shook his head. "I don't think I'm going to." Then he smiled and said, "Hey, want to see me?"

I looked at my watch. A whole minute had gone by. But it wouldn't take long to go with him, and I still felt bad about how I'd treated him at first. "Sure."

"This way. I'm right down the hall."

I followed Scott to a room. Boy. I thought I was hooked up to a lot of stuff. Scott made me look like a free kid. He was wired all over the place. There were two people sitting in the room, looking real sad and holding hands.

"Are those your parents?" I asked.

Scott nodded. "Yeah." He pointed at the woman and said, "That's my mom." Then he pointed to the man and said, "That's my dad."

I guess little kids like to point out stuff. Before we'd gone into the room, he seemed happy. Now, he looked pretty sad. I had an idea. "Hey, I'm going to go outside for a while. Want to come with me?"

Scott looked at his parents. Then he looked at me. "I've been here for days and days. I haven't gone anywhere. Yeah. Come on. Let's go."

"Great." It would be nice to have someone to talk to, even if it was just a little kid.

"Were those your parents back there?" Scott asked.

"Yeah. And Angelina and Norman and Sebastian. But his friends call him Splat," I said.

"Why?" Scott asked.

"It's pretty silly," I told him. "And he doesn't think anybody knows. But I heard my mom telling Mrs. Nissman at the bakery all about it, so I know the whole story. When Sebastian was really little, whenever he needed his diaper changed, he'd jump up in the air so he came down on his rear end."

"Gross," Scott said.

"Yeah. Pretty gross. When he hit the ground, the diaper would make a sound like *splat*. After a while, Sebastian started to shout, 'Splat!' when he jumped. He'd do that until Mom came and changed him. So Mom used to call him her little Splatty-bottom. That turned into Splat-bottom. By the time she stopped, other kids had started calling him Splat, even if they didn't know the reason."

"That's really stupid," Scott said.

I shrugged. "Yeah. I guess it is. Come on — let's get out of here."

"Where are we going?" Scott asked as we walked down the hall.

I realized I couldn't tell him. It wasn't a secret. It was just that I had no idea. No idea at all.

CHAPTER 14
OUT AND ABOUT

We walked down to the door by the stairs. "I wonder what would happen if we went out up here?" Scott said.

"What do you mean?"

"You know. Walked through this wall," he said, pointing to the wall at the end of the hall.

"I guess we'd fall," I said. "But so what? We can't get hurt."

"Let's find out." Scott rushed ahead. I ran to catch up with him. We both went through at the same time.

We fell. But it wasn't fast. It was like we were two leaves floating down. I found out I could spin. I stuck my arms out and pretended I was a helicopter. I can make a really great helicopter sound with my tongue.

"That was fun," Scott said. "Let's do it again."

"How about we do it later," I said. "I really want to get going."

"Okay," Scott said.

I stood on the ground outside the hospital and tried to figure out where to go. "What's a good place for ghosts?" I asked Scott after I'd been thinking for a whole two minutes without getting anywhere.

"I know," he said. "How about the graveyard?"

"NO WAY!" I felt a chill run through me when he said that. I shook my head real hard to try to get rid of the thought. "The haunted house was bad enough," I told him.

"Haunted house?" he asked.

I told him about the Winston House.

"Spooky!" he said when I was done. "Can we go there?"

"Nope. There has to be someplace else." I started walking. I didn't know where I was going, but I figured walking was better than standing still.

We walked for an hour. We saw three other ghosts — all adults. I tried talking to each of them, but it wasn't any use.

"Boy, big people don't pay any attention to kids," Scott said.

"Yeah. Tell me about it. But how come there aren't more ghosts?" I asked.

"What do you mean?"

"Shouldn't there be thousands of ghosts? Maybe

millions?" I wondered why the whole place wasn't filled with ghosts.

"I don't know," Scott said.

I thought about it. I remembered how I'd started to float up when my body was almost all dead. Maybe people didn't stay ghosts for long, except some people. Maybe most people weren't ghosts at all. It was too much to think about, and I had something more important to worry about. I still didn't know where to go. I finally told Scott the truth.

"What do you want to find out?" he asked.

"How to get a message to my parents," I told him.

"Are you sure you can do it?" he asked. "I tried and tried to let my parents know I was there."

"Yeah. I'm pretty sure. You hear about ghosts all the time. People see ghosts, and they see things move, and hear things, and all sorts of stuff like that. So it *has* to be possible. If it wasn't, people would never even know about ghosts. Right?"

"I guess," Scott said, but he didn't sound like he was too sure.

"Think about it," I told him. "You hear people talk about baseball all the time, right?"

"Sure," Scott said.

"And there really is baseball."

"Yup." Scott nodded.

"You never hear them talk about mooseball or hamburgerball, do you? Or zoopydoopyball."

"Nope." Scott said.

"That's because they aren't real. But people talk about seeing and hearing ghosts. It's possible. I know it is. I just have to find out how to do it."

"If I got better, I could tell them for you," Scott said. For an instant, he smiled. Then his smile faded and he shook his head. "That won't work. I know I'm not going to get better."

I didn't like hearing him talk that way. "You'll be okay."

He looked toward where the hospital was. I guess talking about himself made him think of his parents. "Rory, would you get mad if I went back?"

"No, I understand." I figured he wanted to be with his parents as much as possible. "Go ahead. Maybe I'll see you later."

"Yeah. Good luck."

"You, too," I said.

Scott turned away from me and walked back toward the hospital.

I was sorry he was leaving. He wasn't bad company for a little kid. He talked a lot, but that was okay. As I watched him go, I thought about another place where I might find some ghosts. There was a small museum in town. It had lots of old stuff. And ghosts seemed to like to hang out around old stuff. There was even a mummy.

Maybe the mummy's ghost was in the museum.

CHAPTER 15

OLD STUFF

I walked over to the museum. It was closed. That didn't matter, since I could go right through the door. But it was dark, and that mattered. There was just one little light on in each room. I really didn't like walking through a dark, empty place. The spookiest part was that my feet didn't make any sound. I think it would have been better if I could have heard footsteps.

When I walked through the room with the swords, I realized something funny. It would have been great to be here by myself if I could touch the stuff. But being a ghost was like being in a store with Mom. "Don't touch anything." That's what she always said. She especially said it when we were in those stores with all the stuff that breaks real easily. Now, here I was with whole rooms full of really cool stuff, all alone, and I couldn't touch any of it.

When I reached the Egyptian part — it was just one room because the museum isn't all that big — I saw him. He was standing right next to the mummy. I mean, he was the ghost of the guy who'd been made into the mummy. He looked like the pictures of Egyptian people I'd seen in this book Angelina had. The best part was that there was nobody else around. He *had* to pay attention to me.

"Hi," I said. I ran up to him. "My name's Rory."

He looked down at me and smiled. This was great. Then he said, "Rory."

"Yeah. That's me," I told him. "I need some help."

He said something.

"What?" I asked. I didn't understand him.

He said something else.

I didn't understand that, either. Then I figured out what the problem was. "You don't know English, do you?" I asked. "You just talk Egyptian. Right? That's because you're an Egyptian mummy."

He smiled at the word *mummy*. Then he said something I understood. "Look at the mummy."

That was better. Finally, I'd found someone who would talk with me. "Yeah. Look at the mummy. That's you."

"Look at the mummy," he said again. "Oh, gross. Oh, cool. Look at the mummy. Attention please. The museum will be closing in five minutes. Look at the mummy. Don't touch."

I realized he was just saying all the stuff he'd

heard people say when they were in the museum. He kept on talking. "I said don't touch. That's it. I've had it. We're leaving. Look at the mummy. Oh, yuck. Eeewwwww."

"Well, thanks," I told him, "but I have to go. Bye." I waved.

He waved back, then said, "I have to go to the bathroom. I gotta go. I gotta go badly."

"No you don't," I said. I walked through the rest of the museum, but there weren't any other ghosts. On the way out, I stopped again to look at the swords. I really wished I could have touched one.

I stood on the steps outside the museum. "It's not fair," I said. I know I say that a lot, but this really wasn't fair. Cool stuff happened to everyone else. Sebastian got to be a vampire, and Angelina got to be a witch. Even Norman got to turn into a wolf. What did I get? I got dead. That's what I got. I got to be lousy, stinking dead. I could walk through stuff. Big deal. And I had no idea where to go or what to do.

I just started walking again. There were some people on the streets — not ghosts, real people. I ran up to a man and shouted, "DON'T YOU SEE ME?"

He looked puzzled for a second, but then he just shook his head and kept walking. I tried again and again. It was no use. If people noticed anything at all, they just shrugged and told themselves it was their imagination. After that, they didn't notice anything.

I felt so invisible. I felt like I didn't exist. It was worse than being a little kid.

I ran up to another woman. Before I could shout anything, I realized that she looked familiar. She also looked very worried. And she was clutching her pocketbook like it held a treasure. Then I remembered, and I knew I had to follow her. Even if there was nothing I could do to help, I still had to go.

THAT'S A SWITCH

I followed the nice lady all the way back to Madam Zonga's. When she got there, she reached in her purse. Then she held up a bundle wrapped in a handkerchief. "I did what you told me," she said. "It's all here. All my money."

"All of it?" Madam Zonga asked.

The woman nodded. Her face was very pale and her lower lip trembled. So did her hand. The corner of the handkerchief wiggled around like a ghost — I mean, like I used to think a ghost looked.

"Good," Madam Zonga said. I could tell she was trying not to act too excited. She was sitting at her table. "You have done well. Now I can remove the curse. Please be seated so we can begin."

I walked behind her. That's when I saw there was another bundle on a small shelf under the table right in front of Madam Zonga. This bundle was wrapped in a white handkerchief, too. It looked just like the bundle the woman had brought. But I'd bet there wasn't any money in it. I'd bet it was filled with cut up pieces of paper or play money or something.

Madam Zonga put a small bowl on top of the real money. Then she lifted the lid from a black box. There were two eggs inside. She picked up one of the eggs. I saw she had something hidden in her hand, too. I felt like I was watching a magic show.

"Observe," she said. She broke the egg into the bowl. She also dropped the thing she was hiding in her hand. It fell into the egg and spread out like red paint. "Yes! Yes!" Madam Zonga shouted. She jumped back in her chair and pointed. "Do you see?"

The woman nodded and clutched the edges of the table with her hands. "Is that the curse?"

"It is a sign of the curse. There is no mistake. That is why your luck has been so bad. Had you not come to me, who knows what misfortunes you might have suffered. But the spirit has told me what to do. He is here. He is in the room right now," Madam Zonga said. She pointed at a corner behind the other woman. When the woman looked, Madam Zonga grabbed the package from the shelf and switched it with the one under the bowl.

"Cheater!" I shouted.

"Now, we lift the curse," Madam Zonga said. She started mumbling and waving her hands. Then she poured the egg out of the bowl, dropping it into a bucket on the floor. "We shall see . . . " she said. She broke another egg into the bowl. "Yes. The curse is gone."

The woman reached for her money. I wondered what would happen when she opened the handkerchief.

"One thing," Madam Zonga said, putting her hand out. "You must keep the package closed for twenty-four hours. Do not open it until then, or the curse will become ten times as strong."

The woman nodded and grabbed her money. But it wasn't her money. The money was in Madam Zonga's lap. "I can't thank you enough," the woman said as she shoved the bundle back into her purse. Then she walked out the door.

"NO!" I shouted. I screamed so loud I thought my head would explode.

That's when everything went crazy.

17

SMASH AND CRASH

*T*he first crash was so loud, I felt like my head was made of glass and someone had dropped a bowling ball on it. The table made the crash by flying straight up in the air and smacking into the ceiling. Madam Zonga's chair flew apart right under her. Pieces shot in all directions. I tried to jump aside, even though I didn't have to. A couple of the pieces went right through me. Madam Zonga was so startled she just sat there for a second like she still had a chair under her. Then she fell flat on her rear. There was stuff on shelves on one wall — candlesticks and vases and boxes. It all shot across the room like bullets, smashing into the other wall.

Everything looked red. Maybe that was the color of anger. Red and hot. Even the air. It was like looking through one of those red glass jars that Mom collects.

"Ahhhhhggg!" Madam Zonga shrieked. She looked up over her head.

I looked up, too. The table was still pushing against the ceiling, like an animal trying to get out of a cage. The plaster was starting to crack. Then, suddenly, the table zoomed back down and smashed against the floor. It went so fast I could hear the air around it go *whoosh*. The legs snapped in half. The tabletop hit the ground with another huge crash, right next to Madam Zonga. She leaped away, but she still didn't get up.

The curtain on the door to the back room ripped off the rod and fluttered toward Madam Zonga. She screamed louder and curled into a ball.

Every lightbulb in the place blew up.

As quickly as it started, it stopped. The redness faded.

I just stood there, looking around at the smashed and broken pieces. Madam Zonga stared at her hand. The bundle of money twitched.

"Wait!" Madam Zonga cried. She raced for the door. Her right foot got stuck in the bucket, but she didn't stop. "Wait! Lady! Come back! You have the wrong handkerchief. You forgot your money." She tore down the street, making a horrible clank with each step as the bucket hit the sidewalk. I guess she was in a hurry to give the money back.

Wow.

I'd never done anything like this in my life. I didn't know how, but I knew for sure that I'd done it. "Rory did it," I said, thinking about how often other people used those words. Yeah, Rory did it big-time.

I know it's bad to break things. Dad is always saying, "Be a thinker, not a fighter." Mom is always saying, "Violence never solved anything." And Mrs. Rubric has about a thousand different ways to tell the class stuff like that.

But Dad watches boxing, and he cheers when one guy hits another. And Mom likes to slam things in the kitchen when she's angry. And Mrs. Rubric — boy, can she whack the blackboard with a yardstick. She does it so hard it makes my ears hurt.

So I knew what I did was bad, but I still couldn't help smiling a little, even though it was also kind of scary. I think good and bad might be like hot and cold. Some things are really hot, like fire, or really cold, like snow. But it's not always easy to tell. If your hands are really really cold, snow sort of feels warm.

I could worry about that later. Right now, I had something more important to think about. I knew that I could move stuff. And that meant I could get a message to Mom and Dad. But I still didn't know how it had happened, except that it had happened when I'd gotten really really angry.

I needed to find some ghosts. They could explain it to me. But when I went out of Madam Zonga's shop, I saw that I didn't need to look for ghosts. The ghosts had found me. Thousands of ghosts.

18

GALLOPING GHOSTS

They were standing all over the sidewalk and the street. Cars and people went right through them, but they all just stood there, staring at me.

"He's the one," someone said.

"Yes, no doubt," someone else said.

I took a step back. "It was an accident," I said. "I didn't mean to break all that stuff." I wondered how ghosts punished a kid who broke stuff. Whatever they did, I was sure I wouldn't like it.

"Let me through," someone called from the back of the crowd. They started moving aside. A ghost came out of the crowd and walked up to me. I recognized him — it was the man from the Winston House who looked like a Pilgrim.

He pointed a finger at me. "Are you responsible for this occurrence?" He raised his hand and pointed at the shop.

I nodded. I wanted to explain that it wasn't my fault, but when I opened my mouth, nothing came out but a little squeak. I knew I was in big trouble.

"Marvelous," the man said. He clapped his hands together. "It's so rare that we find a talented poltergeist."

"A what?" I asked, but my question was drowned out by the crowd. They'd all started talking and shouting. Ghosts were rushing up, crowding around me. Several of them reached out and touched me like I was some sort of good-luck charm.

"Please!" the Pilgrim man shouted. "Give the youngster some room." He bent down and put an arm around my shoulder. "What's your name?" he asked.

"Rory," I told him. "Rory Claypool."

"I am Josiah Winston," he told me. "Patriarch of the Winston family. But let us not talk about me. It is you who brought us here — you and your rare power."

"What power?" I asked.

He stood up and pointed at the shop again. "The fleshsters use the word *poltergeist*," he said.

"Fleshsters?" I was getting even more confused.

Josiah Winston nodded and looked at a woman who was walking down the street, strolling right through a sea of ghosts. I understood — *fleshsters* were what he called real living people. Before I could ask him anything else, he started talking again.

"*Poltergeist* means 'noisy ghost.' It's a German phrase. It's used when objects go flying around a room, or when things get smashed. The way the fleshsters carry on about it, you'd think it was a common occurrence. But no, my young friend, no. It is a very rare power. To set such forces loose is quite a gift. And you, my boy, have that gift. Most of us have no such power."

Behind him, the crowd started to get noisy again. I guess I wasn't the only noisy ghost. But he ignored the others and kept talking. "We have such great limits," he said. "All of us can cause a little fright or sorrow. We can make the fleshsters tingle and shiver a bit."

He looked around, nervously, then said, "At best, we can touch treasured items from our pasts — perhaps imbue them with a moment of animation. But you can do so much more." He put an arm around me again and started walking.

"Where are we going?" I asked.

"Away," he said. "This place is no longer safe. There are those who lurk in the streets, searching for signs of a disturbance. They have instruments that can detect these outbursts. And yours was quite a powerful display. You've set loose ripples that will not go unseen. We must leave."

He hurried me along the sidewalk. Behind us, I heard a siren. I looked back. A van came roaring around the corner so fast it almost tipped over — the same van I'd seen before with the antenna on top. It drove halfway onto the curb, then stopped. A man jumped out — a tall, thin man with a shaggy beard. He was holding something that looked like a big radio with wires all over the place. There was a wand at the end of one of the wires, and he was waving it all around.

"Yes! Yes!" he shouted. "Poltergeist! Look at the readings! I've never seen it so strong." He waved the wand around some more and watched the lights on the machine. As he swung the wand, it pointed toward me for a second. He swept past me, then swung back. "Aha! Yes!" He turned toward us and started running.

The fleshsters — I mean, the people — in the street stared at him like he was crazy. At the same time, all around him, the crowd of ghosts tried to escape. The man slipped the wand into his belt and then reached into a big pocket in his coat. He pulled out something that looked like a jack-in-the-box. When he turned the handle, it made this awful sound.

I realized it was screeching a tune. It was "Pop Goes the Weasel." When the tune reached the place where you'd sing the word *pop*, I saw a ghost next to the man get sucked into the box. The man kept cranking, faster and faster. Each time the tune reached the end, another ghost got sucked inside. They screamed as they vanished beneath the opening at the top.

"This way," Josiah Winston said. He ran through a store, dragging me with him. We raced out the other side and made several turns.

Finally, we went up the hill to the Winston House.

"Who was that?" I asked.

Josiah Winston shook his head. "An annoyance. A pest who disturbs the peace of all decent ghosts. There are many ghost hunters in this world, but this one is the worst. His name is Magzmir Teridakian."

"Teridakian?" That was bad news. I remembered what Zoltan Teridakian had almost done to Norman, and what Husker Teridakian had tried to do to Sebastian. There didn't seem to be any end to Teridakians. Angelina was lucky there wasn't a witch-hunting Teridakian. Maybe there was and we just never found out about him. Maybe he's still heading toward town.

"Fear not," Josiah Winston told me. "We are safe here. The house protects us. You are welcome to stay as long as you desire."

"But . . ." I tried to tell him I didn't want to stay.

He smiled. "Indeed. You are welcome to stay here forever."

Before I could say anything, the door burst open.

RORY THE STAR

I jumped back, expecting to see Teridakian and his ghost-catching machine. But it was nothing to be scared of — just a bunch of ghosts. They filled the room. I guess they had to use the door because this was a ghost house.

They all wanted to talk to me and tell me about themselves. And they all wanted me to show off.

"Do it again," a man said. "Smash something."

"Come with me," an older man said. He grabbed my right wrist. "My business partner cheated me when I was alive. I want you to destroy his office."

"No, with me," a woman said. She grabbed my left wrist. "Come teach my husband a lesson."

"Stop!" Josiah Winston shouted. "Give the lad some room. You'll all get your turn. There's time enough, and more time beyond. You're acting like a bunch of fleshsters."

The two ghosts let go of me. All the ghosts stepped back for a moment, but that didn't last. They couldn't seem to keep away from me. I guess this was what it felt like to be famous. I looked around for the girl — the nice one who had helped me the first time I came here. But I didn't see her. It was just too crowded. In a moment, they were all around me again, pushing and shoving to get close.

I'd never had so much attention in my life. They all wanted to talk to me. But I started to realize that they really didn't want to talk about me. They wanted to talk about themselves.

It all began to sound the same. Half of them just wanted to brag.

I was an important banker. . . .

You wouldn't know it to look at me now, but I was once the loveliest girl in my village. . . .

Yes, I was a great painter. They all copied me. . . .

I climbed many mountains. . . .

. . . I did . . .

. . . I was . . .

. . . I had . . .

. . . I made . . .

The room was filled with I's.

And half of them wanted me to smash something for them. As soon as I finished talking to one ghost, another would push forward and take his place.

Finally, Josiah shouted, "Enough. Give us some peace."

The rest of the crowd grumbled, but they backed away and went out the door.

"Thanks," I said when the last of them had left. "If I had to listen to one more person's life story, I think I'd scream." As soon as I said that, I felt bad. I realized I didn't know anything about the man who had saved me. "What about you?" I asked. "This is your house, right?"

He shook his head. "This house was built long after I died. I am an ancestor of the man who built it. I never lived here. But this," he said, patting the rocking chair he sat in, "was my chair. When it was brought here, I came with it."

"But why are you a ghost?" I asked.

He smiled, then shrugged. "I'm not sure," he told me. He waved his hand toward where the crowd had stood. "Most of them have unfinished business. They left life too soon. But as for me, I don't know why I remain here."

After that, he stopped talking. I thought he was finished, but then he started again. "I wasn't the best man who ever lived. But I certainly wasn't a bad person. I was only really bad one time in my life. Yet here I am. Maybe I expected this. It's funny. We often get exactly what we expect. Notice how we can walk on the ground, but we walk through walls. I think that happens because we expect it to be that way — we expect solid ground. But I can't complain.

I am comfortable, and in good company. Someday, I imagine I'll pass on. But enough about me."

The way he said it, I knew he didn't want to talk about himself anymore. That was okay. I had other questions. "I still don't understand what I did," I told him.

"You released a pure form of energy. It is produced by great emotions — rage, sorrow, fear."

"Can I control it?" I asked.

"In time, perhaps," he said.

"How long?" I was good at learning things. I'd learned to ride a two-wheeler in less than a day. And that was really hard.

"A century or two," he said.

"A century!" I knew how long that was. And it was more time than I had. Time! I looked at my watch. It was seven-fifteen. It was morning already. I'd wasted hours being famous.

"Thanks for helping me," I said. "I have to go."

"But — "

"I have unfinished business," I told him. I ran toward the door.

"Watch out for Teridakian," he called after me.

"I will." I raced down the steps and rushed toward the hospital.

RUNNING OUT OF TIME

When I reached the hospital, I realized I still had no idea what to do. I stood there, watching my family watch my body. Mom and Dad and Sebastian and Angelina were there. So was Norman. A nurse came in and saw Norman. She told him the room was only for family members. Norman started talking to her, using really big words. Finally, the nurse told him he could stay.

Josiah Winston had told me I had poltergeist power. If I got angry enough, I could smash the whole room.

But that wouldn't do any good. That would just destroy stuff and scare people.

Scare people!

I remembered what else Josiah Winston had said: *All of us can cause a little fright or sorrow. We can make the fleshsters tingle and shiver a bit.* I thought about the rest of what he'd said: *At best, we can touch treasured items from our past.*

I searched the room for anything that might be a treasured item. There wasn't much at all. My clothes were in a closet. I checked my pockets. Nothing. There were some flowers on the table next to the bed. Mom had probably bought them at the hospital gift shop. But I didn't see anything of mine that was a treasure. So that wouldn't work.

I'd have to use fright or sorrow. I didn't want to scare them. It wouldn't do any good. But if I could make them really sad, maybe they'd go home. All of my treasures were at home. Maybe I could find some way to show them the berries. It was my only chance.

I hated to make them sadder. They looked sad enough already. It seemed like a rotten thing to do to them. But I couldn't think of anything else, and I didn't want to stay a ghost forever. *Be sad,* I thought.

Nothing happened. They didn't look any different.

Maybe I was doing it wrong. How do you make people sad? I wondered if they'd get sad if I was sad. I looked at myself lying on the bed and tried to be sad. It didn't work. I mean, my body was sick in the hospital, but I felt fine. Then I thought about Scott. That made me sad. He was so young, and he wasn't going to get any better.

The light in the room got dimmer. Everything looked sad and gloomy. Sad made the air dark blue.

"Oh, man, I can't stand it," Sebastian said. He seemed sad. He stood up. "I can't stay here."

"We understand," Mom said. "Why don't you go home for a while."

Sebastian nodded. Everyone else in the room looked real sad, too. But I guess Sebastian was the saddest. Maybe because he was trying the hardest not to show how he felt. I understood. That's how we are — all us guys.

"I'll go with you," Norman said.

They got up and left the room. I was so happy, I shouted, "Yay!" as I rushed out to follow them.

"Your place or mine?" Norman asked when they walked out the front door of the hospital.

"HOME!" I shouted. They had to go home.

"My place," Sebastian said.

"Are you sure?" Norman asked. "Maybe you'd feel better if you were somewhere else."

"Shut up, Norman!" I told him.

Sebastian shook his head. "No. I want to go home." He started to walk down the street.

Norman followed him. I ran ahead, then waited for them to catch up. They were walking so slowly. I looked at my watch. It was seven-forty-five. It wouldn't take long to get home, but there wouldn't be much time left when we got there.

If they didn't stop anywhere on the way, I figured it would all be okay. And there was no reason for them to stop. No reason at all.

Just when I thought that, I heard Norman say, "Mellon alert."

I looked ahead. Right down the street, straight ahead of us, I saw Pit Mellon. He was too small to bully Sebastian and Norman. But he wasn't alone. He was with a bunch of his big brothers.

FIGURING OUT AN ACTION

I saw Lud and Bud and Clem and Clyde walking with Pit. There were a couple of others I didn't recognize. They were probably cousins or uncles. They were real noisy and rough. Clem and Clyde were hitting each other, and Lud kicked a phone pole as he walked past it. Even though they couldn't touch me, I felt like running.

"Let's go around the other way," Sebastian said. "I don't want to mess with them."

"Yeah, they can be okay alone, but they're unpredictable when they travel in herds," Norman said. "We'd better go the long way."

"No!" I tried to grab Norman but my hand shot right through his arm. If they went the long way, they'd never get home in time. I had to do something. I looked at Pit. He had my action figure in his

hand — it was Mousconi from *Swollen Rat People.*
That was the one he'd taken from me at school. I
could feel the anger boiling inside me. Everything
started to turn red. I knew that in a second or two,
the figure would go flying free, smashing into all the
Mellons. Stones and sticks from the ground would go
flying, too. Pit might even go flying. That's how angry I was getting.

I squeezed my fists together. *Calm down, Rory,* I
told myself. This wasn't right. They'd get hurt. Everyone could get hurt. There had to be another way.
Calm down, I told myself again. The red faded away.
I looked at Pit, and I looked at the figure in his hand.
I stared at it and moved closer. Then even closer. I
knew it so well — every part of it. Even the little
marks in the back from when Darling had started to
chew it. It was mine. It belonged to me.

I moved closer.

And then I was inside of it. I was smaller, and
wearing the figure like a suit of armor. I looked up at
the giant face of Pit Mellon. Then I raised a hand and
pointed at him. "Thief," I whispered, even though I
figured he couldn't hear me. I shook my other fist at
him.

There was no way he could hurt me. I was a ghost
inside a piece of plastic. I was still a little scared, but
not as much as before. The fear was fading.

Pit stared down at me, his eyes wide. He opened

his hand. I stomped my foot hard, slamming my heel on his palm. I was so small it couldn't have really hurt him. But it sure got him moving.

Pit screamed. He turned and ran back toward his house. Anyone with half a brain would have dropped me. But Pit held on at first. Then he must have realized what he was doing. He screamed again and threw me.

Mousconi went flying. I popped out and floated to the ground.

"What's wrong, little brother?" Lud Mellon called.

"Something scare you?" Bud Mellon asked.

All the rest of the Mellons chased after Pit. For a moment, I just stayed where I was. I felt a little confused and dizzy. When I looked back, I saw that Norman and Sebastian had decided not to take the long way.

"What do you think got into them?" Norman asked.

"Must have been frightened by the sight of us," Sebastian said. He held up his arm and flexed his muscle.

I looked around for Mousconi. I could use it to give Sebastian a message. But I didn't know where Pit had thrown it. I couldn't take time to search for it. Norman and Sebastian were already on their way again.

There had to be something in the house I could use

to send a message. "Hurry home," I called over my shoulder as I ran ahead of the two of them.

When I reached the yard, I heard barking. Yip was there. He rushed over and wagged his tail at me. "Good boy," I said. I petted him.

He barked again and licked my face.

"I can't play," I told him. "I have to show Sebastian the berries."

Yip looked at me, then suddenly looked next door toward Mr. Nordy's yard. Then he started to rise slowly into the air. It was just like what happened to me before the ambulance came. As he rose, he started to fade.

CHAPTER 22

GET THE MESSAGE?

"What's wrong?" I asked him.

He didn't bark. He didn't look scared. He just kept drifting higher. I jumped up to grab him, but my hands went right through his body, like he had become the ghost of a ghost.

He wasn't only going higher, he was also going toward Mr. Nordy's yard. I ran through the hedge. When I got to the other side, I saw what was happening.

Mr. Nordy was burying something in a hole at the back of his yard, right next to his flower garden. "Sorry, puppy," he said. "I wish you'd had a longer life." Mr. Nordy doesn't talk much. He started to fill the hole back up. Browser whined. I looked over at Mr. Nordy's house. Sheila, the other dog, was there, with a bunch of puppies. I guess Yip was one of the puppies, but he'd died. I also guess his ghost was waiting until he got buried.

"Bye, Yip," I said.

He looked at me one last time and gave a little bark. Ghosts can't understand animals any better than fleshsters — I mean people — can, but I knew what Yip was saying. He was saying, "It's okay." That's all.

And then he was gone.

Ghosts can cry.

But I knew Yip wouldn't want me to stand there and feel sad. I had to save myself, or I'd be drifting up and fading away real soon, too. I ran back to the house and went to my room.

There were a lot of toys on the floor. There were trucks and soldiers and tons of army stuff — even a gas mask that Dad got me. Then I saw something in the corner. I had a bunch of plastic letters. If I could move them, I could spell a message for Sebastian.

I rushed over to the corner. "You dummy," I said, when I remembered that I couldn't spell. How could I tell Sebastian about berries when I couldn't spell *berries*?

But there was berry punch in the fridge! I ran downstairs. This was great. I could look at the carton and see how to spell the word. "Pretty smart," I said when I reached the kitchen.

I stuck my head right into the refrigerator.

"You dummy," I said again. It was dark in the fridge. I couldn't see anything. The light only came on when the door was open.

I heard another door open. Sebastian and Rory came in. They went upstairs. I ran ahead of them. I looked at my watch. It was eight-oh-three. In a few minutes, my body would start getting sicker and sicker. In the hall, I could hear the two of them going into Sebastian's room.

What could I use to give them a message? I tried to move one of the plastic letters, but nothing happened. There were too many toys. I liked all of them, but they weren't treasures.

Oh, no. I could feel something funny. It was starting. My body was getting lighter. Just a little, but it was happening. I didn't want to be alone when it happened. Even if they couldn't see me, I wanted to be with people I knew. I ran to Sebastian's room.

Right inside, taped to the wall, I saw something I treasured.

I pressed myself against the poster of Frankenstein's monster. It had to work.

It did.

I grew. I moved inside. Then I stepped away.

I heard a rip as the monster tore free from the poster. I staggered for a step or two. It's not easy walking when you're made of paper.

"AAAAAAGGGHHHHH!"

That was Sebastian. He backed up into the corner of his room.

"EEEEEEEEIIIII!"

That was Norman.

He stood up, but then he seemed to freeze.

I took a step toward them. They both screamed again. This wasn't going to work. I had to hope they'd follow me. I turned and walked into the hallway.

"It's mass hysteria or some other form of shared delusion," Norman said. "Definitely a temporary form of dementia. We're imagining it. Lack of sleep. Yeah. That's it. Stress and lack of sleep. This is not real. There's no cause for panic."

I looked back at them. Norman was staring at the floor, shaking his head and telling himself in a thousand different ways that he was imagining this. As far as he was concerned, I wasn't real.

Sebastian was staring at me; his eyes were wide, but he didn't look afraid. He looked amazed.

I turned to face him and motioned with my arm. *Follow me,* I thought. *Please follow me.*

If he came, there was a chance. If not, I knew I was out of time.

CHAPTER 23

NOW OR NEVER

Sebastian stepped away from the wall. "It wants us to follow it," he said.

"You can't follow it!" Norman shouted. "Do you want to know why you can't follow it? Because it isn't real. It can't be real. Therefore, you can't follow it. Just close your eyes until it goes away."

I walked down the stairs. Everything looked so strange. The floor was far away. I was used to being my own height. Frankenstein's monster was a lot taller. I glanced back. Sebastian stepped out of his room.

I went to the kitchen and tried to open the door. But my paper hand slipped around the knob.

"I got it," Sebastian said. He reached out and turned the knob for me.

I walked down the steps and shuffled toward the bushes. It's a good thing it wasn't windy — that would have been trouble. I would have been swept away like a kite with a snapped string. I kept looking back to make sure that Sebastian was following me. When I reached the bushes, I leaned over and grabbed at a berry. It wasn't easy with paper fingers but I got one and managed to pull it off.

I turned back to Sebastian and held out the berry.

"What?" he asked. "I don't understand."

I held the berry up to my mouth like I was going to eat it.

"Are you crazy?" Sebastian said. "Don't you know red berries are poisonous?"

"THAT'S WHAT I'VE BEEN TRYING TO TELL YOU!" I shouted. Of course, he didn't hear me.

But he heard himself. "Poisonous!" he said again. "I have to call the hospital." He raced back inside.

I stepped out of the poster. It fluttered to the ground behind me. I followed Sebastian and watched while he called. He told them about the berries. By then, Norman had come down from upstairs.

"Rory will be okay now," Sebastian told him after he hung up. "The doctors are getting him the right medicine. Come on. I want to be there when he wakes up."

So did I. I had a funny feeling that I should be near my body when I woke up. I followed Sebastian and Norman out the front door.

I was so happy, I didn't even notice the van.

Round and round the mulberry bush . . .

All of a sudden, something was pulling me. "Yes, I knew it. There was so much spectral energy here," Teridakian said. He was pointing his ghost grabber at me and cranking the handle. It played that awful music.

I reached for Sebastian. It was no use. My hands went right through his arm. My body was being sucked into Teridakian's machine.

The monkey chased the weasel . . .

"Stop!" I shouted. "Please."

My foot got caught. I was being pulled in. But I felt a pull in another direction. My body, my real body, was trying to pull me back. The doctors were fixing me.

The machine was stronger.

I was more than halfway inside.

Sebastian looked at the van. I guess he read the part about ghost hunters. Then he looked toward me. "Norman, he's got Rory."

"What?" Norman asked.

The monkey thought 'twas all in fun . . .

I was in up to my shoulders. I tried to push myself out, but it was too strong. I knew that as soon as the music reached the word *pop*, I'd be sucked inside for good.

"Stop thinking so much," Sebastian shouted. He ran up to Teridakian and grabbed the ghost-catching machine.

"Hey!" Teridakian shouted. "Give that back."

"No way," Sebastian said. He threw the machine toward Norman. "Get him out. Save him."

Norman caught me. He looked surprised. I think he usually drops anything that's thrown at him.

"Go!" Sebastian shouted.

Norman ran back inside the house with me while Sebastian blocked Teridakian from following.

"Oh, man," Norman said. He pulled something out of his pocket. I twisted my head around so I could see what he had. It was a knife — the kind that has a screwdriver and lots of other stuff.

"Hurry," I said, even though he couldn't hear me. My head felt like it was going to be torn in half. The force pulling at me got stronger and stronger, but I was stuck in the machine.

"Okay, this can't be too hard," Norman said. He removed a screw and took the cover off. "Yes, I got it," he said. I could barely see what he was doing, but it looked like he unhooked some wires and then put them back on.

My neck was starting to stretch. I felt like a giraffe. "Hurry," I shouted.

Sebastian dashed in and slammed the door. Outside, Teridakian was pounding at the door and yelling.

"Did you do it?" Sebastian asked.

"Almost," Norman said. "I tried to crank it backward, but it doesn't go that way. So I reversed the wires between the crank and the motor. Whatever it did before, it will do the opposite now."

My head had stretched so far I could look down and see the machine in Norman's hands.

"Are you sure?" Sebastian asked.

"No. I'm not sure. I could ask the fellow outside who's trying to break your door, but I doubt he's in the mood to discuss electronics with me at the moment. All I can do is hope."

I was sure something was about to break. I couldn't stand another second. "Stop talking!"

Norman cranked the handle.

CHAPTER 24

GREAT EXPECTATIONS

*P*OP *goes the weasel . . .*

As the end of the tune played, I shot out of the machine so fast I felt like a bullet. I went right through the house and over the neighborhood. I guess my body was pulling real hard.

I zoomed straight through the hospital. As I was flying into my room, I saw Scott in the hallway.

"Hi, Rory," he called as I flashed by.

"Scott," I shouted. There was something I had to tell him. Something I'd learned. But there was hardly any time. "Stop expecting — "

I'd just barely said that much when I got pulled back into me. I'd wanted to tell him that he should stop expecting to die. I remembered how he told me he wasn't going to live. But I'd learned that what you expect can change things. Not always, but sometimes.

I was back in me. Everything went away for a while. Then I woke up. Mom and Dad and everyone was there. They were all hugging me and crying, except Sebastian, who was pretending not to cry.

"That was you in the poster, right?" Sebastian whispered to me.

"Yeah."

He sighed. "Phew. That's a relief."

I guess he was glad it wasn't some other ghost. Mom said we'd talk about the television later. That was going to be some talk. But I didn't mind. Whatever my punishment was, I could take it.

Norman was there, too. "Thanks," I said to him when my parents weren't listening.

"Any time," he said. "I like a challenge."

"What about Teridakian?" I asked him. "What happened after I left?"

Norman grinned. "I gave him back his machine and he drove off. I didn't tell him the wires were reversed. He'll never catch another ghost."

The doctor said I could go home. He gave me a lecture about not eating strange berries. I promised him I wouldn't ever do that again. I got dressed. Then I looked at the flowers on the table next to the bed.

"I needed to cheer up the way the room looked," Mom said. "I bought them last evening. But I forgot to put them in water. I guess they died."

"That's okay," I said. "They're still nice." I grabbed the flowers.

They made me ride in a wheelchair. They don't like to let people walk out of a hospital. I don't understand that. But as we were going down the hall, I heard something terrible. I told the nurse to stop.

I looked into the room we were passing. It was Scott's room. His mom and dad were crying. I guess he hadn't understood my message. As good as I felt for myself, I felt terrible for Scott.

His mother sobbed again, then said, "It's a miracle."

I realized she was crying because she was so happy. Adults do that. She was sobbing and holding onto Scott. He was sitting up.

"The doctor said you'll be fine now," Scott's dad said. "No more hospitals."

Scott lifted his head from his mother's shoulder. He smiled at me and said, "Hi, Rory."

"Hi, Scott," I said. "You got better."

"I expected to," he said.

"Do you know him?" Mom asked as they rolled me down the hall.

"We've met," I told her.

As we reached the elevator, I heard Scott calling again from his room. "Hi, Splat-bottom," he said. Then he laughed. We were far enough away that I don't think anyone else heard him very clearly. But

Sebastian frowned and looked over his shoulder toward Scott's room.

We got out of the hospital, went to the car, and started for home. We drove the long way, because Mom wanted to pick up some milk.

"Dad, can you stop here for a second?" I asked as we came down the hill.

"Sure." He sounded puzzled, but he did it.

"I'll be right back." I grabbed the flowers and ran up the porch of the Winston House.

"Here you go," I said. I put the flowers down right in front of the door. I hoped the girl would see them. Maybe when flowers died, they became ghosts. I didn't know. But it still made me feel good.

"Ready to go home?" Dad asked when I got back into the car.

"I sure am," I told him. "All I want to do is curl up on the couch and watch some — "

I stopped. I was just about to say *television*.

Mom put a hand on my shoulder. "We'll get it fixed. But for tonight, how about I read you a book?"

"That sounds great," I said. "As long as it's not a ghost story."

Sebastian laughed and poked me on the shoulder. It felt good. It felt wonderful.

I liked being a fleshster.

AUTHOR'S NOTE

I really enjoyed writing about Rory's adventures. The idea of a young ghost in a world filled with adult ghosts was exciting. It came to me a long time ago, but I carried it inside of me while I wrote the other books in this series. Part of me was almost afraid to start writing, for fear the story wouldn't come. But it came. And it told itself well. I'm pleased with it. If you like to write, pay special attention to those ideas that make you shiver with excitement. Watch for the ideas that are so wonderful you absolutely have to put them down on paper. Trust yourself.

I couldn't even begin to pretend that I wrote these four tales of The Accidental Monsters all by myself with no help, assistance, support, or encouragement. I need to thank a lot of wonderful people. The time has come. Here goes.

Thanks to Joelle and Alison at home, and Jon down

South. Thanks to Ashley and Carolyn Grayson, Dan Hooker, and Jace Foss at the agency. Thanks to Tonya Martin at Scholastic. Thanks to Dian Curtis Regan and Marilyn Singer, both on the Net and in the real world. Thanks to Lorraine Stanton, Kathy Belby, and Nancy McMichael, critiquers past and present. Thanks to Fred and Adrienne Fedorko, down the block. And to Doug Baldwin and Connie Cook down the road. Special thanks to Fern Baldwin for many great suggestions and a fine critical eye. Thanks to Chris Jarocha-Ernst for feedback and support. My deepest thanks to the staff and students of Lower Nazareth Elementary School for being so wonderful, for loving books, and for letting me use them as a practice audience.

Phew. That just leaves you, my marvelous reader. I can't thank you enough. I hope you enjoyed yourself as much as I did. Keep an eye out for me. I've got more tales to tell.

THE ACCIDENTAL MONSTERS

POOF! You're a Vampire! ZAP! You're a Witch!

Find out what's in store for you next. Don't miss these other Accidental Monsters books!

APPLE® PAPERBACKS

Pick an Apple and Polish Off Some Great Reading!

BEST-SELLING APPLE TITLES

❏ MT43944-8	**Afternoon of the Elves** Janet Taylor Lisle	**$2.99**
❏ MT41624-3	**The Captive** Joyce Hansen	**$3.50**
❏ MT43266-4	**Circle of Gold** Candy Dawson Boyd	**$3.50**
❏ MT44064-0	**Class President** Johanna Hurwitz	**$3.50**
❏ MT45436-6	**Cousins** Virginia Hamilton	**$3.50**
❏ MT43130-7	**The Forgotten Door** Alexander Key	**$2.95**
❏ MT44569-3	**Freedom Crossing** Margaret Goff Clark	**$3.50**
❏ MT42858-6	**Hot and Cold Summer** Johanna Hurwitz	**$3.50**
❏ MT25514-2	**The House on Cherry Street 2: The Horror**	
	Rodman Philbrick and Lynn Harnett	**$3.50**
❏ MT41708-8	**The Secret of NIMH** Robert C. O'Brien	**$3.99**
❏ MT42882-9	**Sixth Grade Sleepover** Eve Bunting	**$3.50**
❏ MT42537-4	**Snow Treasure** Marie McSwigan	**$3.50**
❏ MT42378-9	**Thank You, Jackie Robinson** Barbara Cohen	**$3.99**

Available wherever you buy books, or use this order form

Scholastic Inc., P.O. Box 7502, 2931 East McCarty Street, Jefferson City, MO 65102

Please send me the books I have checked above. I am enclosing $_____ (please add $2.00 to cover shipping and handling). Send check or money order—no cash or C.O.D.s please.

Name_____Birthdate_____

Address_____

City_____State/Zip_____

Please allow four to six weeks for delivery. Offer good in U.S. only. Sorry mail orders are not available to residents of Canada. Prices subject to change.   APP596